The Lady in White

The Hellion Club, Novella

by Chasity Bowlin

Text by Chasity Bowlin
Cover by Dar Albert

Originally published as *Once Upon a Haunted Garden* in the 2023 Dragonblade Publishing anthology Once Upon a Haunted Romance.

Dragonblade Publishing, Inc. is an imprint of Kathryn Le Veque Novels, Inc.
P.O. Box 23
Moreno Valley, CA 92556
ceo@dragonbladepublishing.com

Produced in the United States of America

First Edition October 2024
Print Edition

ARE YOU SIGNED UP FOR DRAGONBLADE'S BLOG?

You'll get the latest news and information on exclusive giveaways, exclusive excerpts, coming releases, sales, free books, cover reveals and more.

Check out our complete list of authors, too!

No spam, no junk. That's a promise!

Sign Up Here

www.dragonbladepublishing.com

Dearest Reader;

Thank you for your support of a small press. At Dragonblade Publishing, we strive to bring you the highest quality Historical Romance from some of the best authors in the business. Without your support, there is no 'us', so we sincerely hope you adore these stories and find some new favorite authors along the way.

Happy Reading!

CEO, Dragonblade Publishing

Additional Dragonblade books by Author Chasity Bowlin

The Hellion Club Series

A Rogue to Remember (Book 1)
Barefoot in Hyde Park (Book 2)
What Happens in Piccadilly (Book 3)
Sleepless in Southampton (Book 4)
When an Earl Loves a Governess (Book 5)
The Duke's Magnificent Obsession (Book 6)
The Governess Diaries (Book 7)
A Dangerous Passion (Book 8)
Making Spirits Bright (Novella)
All I Want for Christmas (Novella)
The Boys of Summer (Novella)
When The Night Closes In (Novella)
The Lady in White (Novella)

The Lost Lords Series

The Lost Lord of Castle Black (Book 1)
The Vanishing of Lord Vale (Book 2)
The Missing Marquess of Althorn (Book 3)
The Resurrection of Lady Ramsleigh (Book 4)
The Mystery of Miss Mason (Book 5)
The Awakening of Lord Ambrose (Book 6)
Hyacinth (Book 7)
A Midnight Clear (Novella)

The Lyon's Den Series

Fall of the Lyon
Tamed by the Lyon
Lady Luck and the Lyon

The Lyon, the Liar and the Scandalous Wardrobe

Pirates of Britannia Series

The Pirate's Bluestocking

Also from Chasity Bowlin

Into the Night (Novella)

Chapter One

August 28th, 1832

THE LIBRARY AT Rosehaven Manor was awe-inspiring, filled to the brim with leather-bound volumes and priceless artifacts. Miss Louisa Jones's fingers itched to touch them. But, as per her training, she remained seated before the dark and somewhat brooding master of the house, her hands folded primly in her lap and her posture perfect. It was an interview for a position, after all. One that she had gotten entirely on her own, for that matter. She needed to know that she could manage her life without Effie's assistance. Oh, Effie would never withdraw her aid. But it was a matter of pride for Louisa to prove that she could do it without her mentor's influence.

"Your references are most excellent, Miss Jones," Mr. Blackwell mused. He seemed less than pleased about it, strangely.

She felt herself blushing under his regard. From her first sight of him, she'd felt strangely breathless and, while the phrase did not adequately convey her feelings, out of sorts. He was a ridiculously appealing man. His features, on the whole, were not what would be called handsome, and yet he was arresting. His face was all sharp planes and angles with deep obsidian eyes, and his dark hair that waved away from his face in a casual disarray implied he was not bothered by vanity. But then, he didn't need to be. He wasn't the sort who would have to put in very much effort to appeal to women.

"Thank you, sir. You are very kind to say so."

He placed the letters back on the inlaid top of the desk. "You will not think me kind for very long, Miss Jones. Despite your excellent references, I'm afraid you have wasted your journey here."

Louisa's polite smile faltered. "I beg your pardon?"

He folded the papers all together, then bundled them back into the small folio before shoving them across the surface of the desk toward her. "I am terribly sorry that you've come all this way. You'll be compensated for your time and expense, and I shall arrange lodging for you at the local inn until transportation back to London can be obtained."

It was much more than simply choosing another candidate, Louisa thought. That was a very decisive dismissal. She had offended him somehow. It was the only possible explanation. But how? They'd barely spoken. "My apologies, Mr. Blackwell. I was under the impression that the position was already mine and this interview was simply a formality."

"I'm afraid my man of affairs, Mr. Hatton, was a bit presumptuous, but alas . . . we would not suit, Miss Jones," he answered firmly.

"Isn't it more important that your aunt and I suit one another?" she demanded. Her tone was no longer polite. There was a decided snap to it. But it couldn't be helped. The sting of humiliation, to be summed up and dismissed without even offering her a chance, was unbearable. Under the circumstances, she found her control of her behavior with such charged emotions quite impressive.

His dark eyebrows lifted with incredulity. "My aunt?"

"Yes. That is why I am here, after all—to be interviewed for the position of companion to your spinster aunt, Miss Mary Blackwell. Isn't it?"

His demeanor shifted instantly. She'd heard people refer to a man's expression as thunderous before, but she didn't believe she'd ever seen anything that actually fit the description so well. He was furious.

The words were bitten out, his jaw clenched tightly. "There appears to be some miscommunication, Miss Jones. I am not seeking a companion for my aunt."

"Then what is the position, Mr. Blackwell?"

He stared at her for a moment without speaking. He'd once more schooled his face into a mask of impassivity, and whatever he was thinking or feeling was simply unknown to her, hidden in the depths of that dark gaze. The silence, however, was grim. At long last, he ground out the words, "My wife, Miss Jones. Mr. Hatton was to find me a suitable candidate for marriage."

Louisa could not have been more shocked. "You cannot possibly be considering seeking a wife in such a fashion!"

"I am," he stated. "I gave Mr. Hatton very specific requirements, and he has chosen to ignore them all."

She didn't flinch. Even if everything inside her recoiled at that slight, she knew better than to allow any outward display of her misery. It wasn't as if she wanted to marry him. He was practically a Bedlamite, it seemed. But rather, his immediate dismissal of her, as if she didn't even warrant consideration, was a reminder of all the many times in her life when those around her found her lacking.

Oblivious, he continued, "Please wait here while I speak to Mr. Hatton and get to the bottom of this." Then he rose from his desk and stormed out.

Alone, Louisa deflated in the chair. Her posture was no longer rigidly straight as befitted the comportment of a graduate of the Darrow School. Instead, she slumped, her shoulders rounding with defeat and her chin dropping to her chest dejectedly. But that only lasted for a moment. She'd be going back to London with her proverbial tail tucked between her legs, but that didn't mean she would simply sulk like a spoiled child because she didn't get her way. Instead, she rose. With no need to worry about the sort of impression she was making, she gave free rein to her curiosity. Getting up, she strode toward the shelves and began to examine the ancient artifacts displayed there. Since she wasn't getting the job, there was no reason to worry about what he might think of her.

One item in particular piqued her interest. It was a bronze dagger. Lifting it, she marveled at the weight of it as she turned it over and over in her hand. It was a lovely piece, not Roman or Greek, but Norse, she imagined, based on the carvings.

She was just about to replace it on the shelf when she felt it. A mere whisper of wind moving across the back of her neck, ruffling the fine hairs that had slipped from her chignon despite her attempts to tame them.

A breeze, her mind insisted. But it was August. And in the wake of that current of air, her skin was ice cold.

"A COMPANION?" DOUGLAS demanded as he paced the drawing room. "That is what you told this poor girl who has traveled so far from her home?"

Mr. Hatton held up his hands in mock supplication. "I could hardly place an advertisement or contact an agency and ask them to send prospective brides to interview for the position of Mrs. Blackwell, could I? And the girl doesn't have a home. Not really. She's a graduate of the Darrow School and resides there until such time as she can obtain suitable employment . . . or another proper situation."

Douglas shoved his hands into his hair in frustration. The young woman currently in his library was a complication he had not counted on. Hatton had been entrusted with a simple task: find a plain woman with no prospects who would happily marry him and after their requisite year as husband and wife, live entirely separate from him. She would be able to content herself with the financial security their arrangement would afford her. Miss Louisa Jones was not the sort to be satisfied with such things. And if he married her, letting her entirely walk away would be an impossibility. Just seeing her as she'd entered the room had created an awareness in him that he knew could only be disastrous.

He'd lived his entire life with caution, with an awareness that when the men of the Blackwell family allowed their emotions to hold sway, only disaster and tragedy would follow. He could not afford any sort of entanglement, even an honorable one, with a woman who so thoroughly entranced him.

"Hatton, you know why I insisted on a plain and unassuming spinster for a bride! I will not damn some innocent young woman to the terrible fate that so many women meet when they have the misfortune to marry into this family!"

The older man's face flushed and he looked away, unable to meet Douglas's gaze. "That is superstitious nonsense, sir. You are not like your uncle. Not at all."

"Not yet," Douglas replied. "Not yet. But am I like my grandfather? Or my grandfather before him? It isn't just my uncle, as you well know! Historically speaking, there is only one way this will play out. I will not wager that young woman's life on it."

Hatton shook his head. "You haven't the time to be choosy. You had one year from the date of your uncle's death to take a wife or forfeit the fortune. With only a few short weeks remaining, finding another prospective bride will not be easy. In fact, it might well be impossible!"

Douglas paced the length of the drawing room. "There are local women—"

"Who know the history of this family and this place, or think they know it," Hatton pointed out. "They would never consent."

Douglas cursed under his breath. It was true enough. Half the people in the village wouldn't even look at him. Those that would did so with blatant hostility. His options were limited. "Damn it all."

"She is made of much sterner stuff than you imagine, sir. Miss Jones is no milk and water society miss. That young woman has a spine of forged steel and a character that is just as firm," Mr. Hatton stated. "Take a chance. It's your only option, really."

Douglas watched the older man walk away, victorious in his fait accompli. With the weight of the world on his shoulders, he turned and made his way back to his library where Miss Jones was no longer simply waiting patiently. Instead, she was holding an ancient bronze dagger, part of his uncle's extensive collection of antiquities, examining it as though she were the expert curator of a museum rather than a young woman trapped between the serving and upper class.

Her dark auburn hair was pulled back in a severe fashion, though strands of it were fighting her efforts admirably. For a moment, he let himself imagine the texture of it. Like silk, he thought. Like her hairstyle, her drab gray gown was intended to be functional only and not in the least flattering. None of that could disguise her beauty. He fervently prayed that he was not on the cusp of making a terrible mistake.

"Miss Jones, there is a matter of some confusion that must be cleared up prior to our discussing your future here at Rosehaven Manor," he said.

She looked back at him, startled. "I wasn't aware I had a future at Rosehaven Manor, sir. You had made that abundantly clear."

"What I made clear was that you would not be my aunt's companion. That remains true. But the other position, the more permanent one, upon reflection seems to be the best course of action. I realize you came here expecting to be hired as a companion, but I'd very much like to ask you to remain at Rosehaven . . . as my wife."

Chapter Two

LOUISA NEARLY DROPPED the ancient artifact she held. "You cannot be serious. Only moments ago, you stated—and rather firmly, I might add—that I was not suitable."

"I have reconsidered my stance, and my opinion has altered significantly," he replied.

"I will not be made fun of this way!" Louisa could feel her face flaming with indignation. The whole business reminded her of the cruel teasing she'd endured as a young child. Offers of friendship had been extended simply to lure her into a situation where she could be humiliated before everyone. "It's one thing to have brought me here at great expense and difficulty; it is quite another to laugh at me in the process."

"I am not making fun of you. I can assure you, Miss Jones, that the offer is very real," he said. "My intentions are honorable. If you would permit me to explain?"

Reluctantly, Louisa nodded. She didn't trust herself to respond verbally.

"My uncle, whom I inherited Rosehaven from, died nearly a year ago. I was still with the army then. Between the difficulties in resigning my commission and the lengthy journey home, the year that he allotted for me to find myself a bride has nearly gone. While you are not the sort of young lady I imagined marrying, you are the only one to whom I can be wed in the amount of time I have left—if I fail, all is forfeit. Not the house, because it is entailed, but the fortune with which to sustain it will go to a cousin, who will then have one year to find a bride, and so on . . . until it reaches someone down the line of inheritance that is already married or willing to become so."

Louisa's eyebrows rose nearly to her hairline. She'd never been so insulted in her life. Given that she'd lived a good portion of her young life either in the rookeries or on the street, that was certainly saying something. "So I'm not what you want, but I'll do?"

He sighed, a sound of frustration and, she could only imagine, disappointment. "I am explaining this all very badly. Had Mr. Hatton been more forthcoming about my reasons, this might have been avoided. I specifically told him to seek a spinster with limited prospects. Someone who would not balk at the sort of arrangement I am offering."

"I am a spinster with limited prospects," she insisted.

"On that point I must beg to differ. No woman, Miss Jones, who looks as you do is ever without prospects."

Louisa blushed furiously under the weight of his regard. He looked at her in a way that she understood, a way that many men had looked at her in her life. But she'd never enjoyed their attentions. With him, it was another matter altogether.

"But what sort of arrangement?"

"We will live here as man and wife, with all that entails, for one year. Long enough to meet the terms of the will. Then we will part and live very separate lives."

Louisa could not imagine any man making such a choice. "Why? Why would you choose such an arrangement?"

He shrugged. "I dislike disorder, Miss Jones. I prefer my life to be regimented, dull, boring, and entirely uneventful. I seek to avoid anything that will spike my temper or even positive feelings. Emotional upheaval is to be avoided at all cost."

Lies. At the very minimum, what he'd offered was certainly no better than a half truth. "And you think I would cause you *emotional upheaval*?"

"Not intentionally. The failing lies entirely with me, Miss Jones. I am well aware of how peculiar all of this is. But my time is limited. And while you do not meet the parameters I set forth for Mr. Hatton, I would still offer you this opportunity. It could mean a life without being in servitude to anyone else."

"But no chance for love or even contentment in marriage," she pointed out. There was a hint of response. A slight tightening of his jaw that made her wonder if perhaps what he'd described wasn't what he wanted but what he thought he should have. "What about children?"

"There will be no children. The marriage will be consummated so that no one can challenge its legitimacy, but precautions will be taken." He didn't elaborate, and she hadn't the nerve to ask. So he continued, "In return for your sacrifices, you would have financial security, an elevated position in society, and a kind of independence few married ladies—or unmarried ladies, for that matter—enjoy. I will have a room prepared for you, Miss Jones. You will remain here for the night and you may consider the offer. If you choose to accept it, I will obtain a common license and we shall wed immediately. If you elect to disdain this offer, I will arrange for your transportation back to London and see that you are well compensated for your time."

He sketched a slight bow, then turned on his heel and left. Once more, she was alone in the library. With the dagger still in her hand, she turned and replaced it carefully on the shelf. On unsteady legs, she returned to the chair she'd occupied before. How she wished she could talk to Effie! Or even Alexandra. The young girl had become a confidant of sorts over the years. Of course, given Alexandra's obsession with gothic novels, her opinion could hardly be counted. The whole thing sounded remarkably like the plot of one of her fanciful books!

What am I going to do? It was insanity to even consider it. But he'd offered her something that she had craved throughout her life. Not simply independence or security—but independence *with* security. To have financial security without having to work for others was a fantasy for most young women of her class. She could hardly imagine what it would be like to live her life with no threat of being sacked at the whim of a capricious employer. No fighting off unwanted advances. No bowing and scraping in the face of unreasonable demands. She could have her dignity and her pride as well as a roof over her head. And all she'd have to sacrifice was the possibility of things she might never have anyway—or worse, things that never lasted and only led to bitterness and heartache.

Chapter Three

LOUISA HAD AWAKENED from a fitful sleep. The air was still and thick in her chamber. The curtains at the open window did not flutter at all. And yet her skin was ice cold. The sensation was so similar to what she'd experienced earlier in the library that she knew it could not be simply her imagination.

Alexandra, if she were there, would blame it on a spirit. And perhaps it was, but Louisa wasn't brave enough to call out to it in the dark of night. Instead, she lay there in her bed, willing the sensation to go away. At long last, it did—the cold receded. No. It did not recede. Rather, it moved away from her. It didn't simply dissipate. It moved over her body like a caress.

The shiver that racked her was not born of that cold but of fear. What was it? If it were a spirit, what could it possibly want with her?

The absurdity of it all was too much. "It's not a spirit. Such things are nothing more than fiction," she said aloud, her voice barely more than a whisper. "It's been a trying day with a great deal of . . . *upheaval*. You are overwrought and questioning the decisions you have made."

And she had made her decision, if one could even term it that.

Married. But not really married. A wife for one year, and then a wife in name only. She had accepted Mr. Blackwell's proposal and would be his bride—living in his home for one year.

However much she might have weighed it, measured it, and

turned it over and over in her mind for dozens of times that day, she was still confounded by it all. Each time, she had come up with the same answer. It was the best opportunity she'd ever be presented with in her life. And she wasn't about to let a drafty house and an overactive imagination get the better of her.

When she'd come to Kent seeking employment, she'd never imagined that the course of her future might be altered so dramatically. While it wasn't something every girl dreamed of, it was something that a girl such as herself—one who had known the misery of true poverty—could not ignore. Even if it wasn't in the normal way of things, it was still beyond anything she might have imagined for her future. But it wasn't the wealth, the position, or even the very enigmatic man to whom she'd found herself betrothed. Instead it was that indefinable feeling which she sometimes had, an intuition of sorts that led her down the paths she was supposed to go. It was that same feeling she'd had when presented with the option to attend the Darrow School on Effie's charitable nature. She'd known it was the right thing to do instantly. It had been the same with the proposal. Rational arguments aside, she'd heard that voice inside her urging her in that direction.

But now, in the dark hours of the night, alone in the great house save for the servants two floors above and an elderly woman at the opposite end of the corridor, one she had yet to even meet—and her prospective husband, wherever he might be—that certainty wavered. Doubts crept in, along with dozens of questions. Not least of which was why a man who was handsome, well connected, and on the verge of being incredibly wealthy would need to marry a woman with no pedigree and nothing beyond a grasp of etiquette and decorum to recommend her. The nonsense he'd uttered about wanting an orderly life rang hollowly. Men who truly wanted an orderly life got themselves a wife to make it so. To marry and then just eschew it to live like a bachelor—it was nonsensical.

Rolling from her side and onto her back, she stared up at the canopied ceiling of the bed. She was wrestling as much with the decision she had made as with the prospect of informing Effie what she had done. And she was wrestling with the realities of being married to a man she knew nothing of.

In the end, the mystery of whatever the problem was that required such a drastic solution pricked at her mind in a way that left her decidedly unsettled. Too unsettled to even think of sleep.

Pushing back the sheet, she rose and padded on bare feet to the window. There, she looked out at the garden below. Movement caught her eye, and as she turned her head to see what it was, her breath caught. She blinked, rubbing her eyes to be certain that they were not deceiving her.

A wraith-like mist moved through the garden. Stark white against the darkness, it drifted to and fro, winding around hedges and bushes in a serpentine fashion until it simply vanished. There was no gait. No steps. It appeared to simply float until it vanished beyond the hedgerow where it flanked the lane.

"It is a mere trick of the light," she whispered to herself. "Nothing more. There are no phantoms here . . . nor anywhere else." And yet, even as she backed away from the window and retreated to the confines of her bed, she was not fully convinced of that fact. Certainly not as convinced as she ought to have been.

A cold chill snaked over her skin, despite the oppressive heat. And yet it was different from the cold sensation she'd experienced before. This came from within. A warning from her own intuition. It was accompanied by a sense of foreboding. There were ominous goings-on afoot—not ghostly, but ominous—at Rosehaven Manor. What they might mean for her future there was as yet unknown.

"Please let me know if I have made a terrible mistake," she whispered in nearly silent prayer against her pillow. "Let this not be the first time my intuition leads me astray."

IT WAS MID-MORNING when he returned. He'd left at first light to make all the necessary arrangements. Now, Douglas bore the common license tucked inside his coat as he led his mount up the graveled drive and toward the hulking shape of Rosehaven Manor. But he hadn't reached the house when he drew up short. There was a lone figure walking along the lane. No phantom, but a flesh and blood woman who was poking and prodding at the bushes with a stick. *His betrothed.* Miss Louisa Jones.

"Did you lose something?" he asked, as he neared her.

She looked back at him, wide eyed. There was a leaf stuck in her hair. "No, I . . . well, I was just admiring the foliage."

Lie. That was immediately apparent. Why? And then it simply came to him. Had she heard the stories of the White Lady of Rosehaven? Or had she seen her? "Foliage," he mused. "Or perhaps some remnant of a white gown trapped in the brush?"

Her guilty flush was confirmation. With a heavy sigh, Douglas dismounted and approached her. "Did you see Rosehaven's infamous phantom, Miss Jones?"

"I saw something," she countered. "I do not believe in phantoms."

Her reasonable response was not unexpected, but it was very welcome. It was also not entirely convincing. But Rosehaven was no place for anyone given to hysterics. "Perhaps I can aid you in your search, or answer any questions you may have about what you saw."

"What I *thought* I saw," she stressed. "It was very late, or very early depending upon one's perspective. It was very warm last night, so I moved to the window hoping for a breeze. There was someone walking through the garden and then along the lane here. Wearing white."

"Someone. Not something?"

Her lips firmed into a thin hard line, her expression revealing just how dubious she found that option. "I realize that many people are given to flights of fancy and succumb to superstitious notions. I am not one of those people, sir."

"Indeed, I can see that you are not. I would caution you, Miss Jones, about asking too many questions to servants or to those in the village—assuming they would speak with you at all," he said. "The Blackwell family is not thought very kindly of here. You will find that out soon enough."

"You make it sound as if they see you as some sort of villain!" she protested.

"Not me, Miss Jones. All the Blackwells, but specifically any who reside at Rosehaven. Our history with the village is not a pleasant one, and they are entitled to view us as such. You will not receive a warm welcome there, I am afraid."

"My lord, I am the illegitimate child of the disgraced daughter of a baronet. My mother's family has refused to acknowledge me, and my father's family is entirely unknown to me. I have not been warmly welcomed anywhere. I daresay that I will survive their snubs," she answered.

Her tone was matter-of-fact, her delivery of that sad statement revealing the pragmatism that was likely responsible for her decision to agree to his proposal. "Yet you have thrived, Miss Jones. Where most would have crumbled, you have risen above your humble origins."

"They are less than humble. Some would even call them ignoble," she pointed out. "Most people in the upper classes tend to frown upon those in the lower classes rising above anything."

It wasn't an accusation, but simply an observation. And it was an observation he could not refute. "Perhaps my years in the army, seeing more of the world than simply what exists here, has given me a more egalitarian view of things."

"Perhaps it has," she mused. "So who is this phantom people speak of?"

"Her name is unknown," he replied. "But for the last century, there have been tales of her wandering the grounds here and even being seen in the village. The White Lady of Rosehaven is presumed to be the tragic love of one of my ancestors . . . a woman who paid the ultimate price for loving unwisely."

"Or the guise of a phantom affords young women an opportunity to sneak about at night without anyone being the wiser," she countered.

A smile tugged at Douglas's lips. "You are very suspicious of your own sex."

"I've lived in a school with other girls for the past decade. I know precisely how sneaky we can be. I also know we have no choice but to be sneaky because so many limitations are placed on us by society," she pointed out. "Such ruses are not unheard of."

"No, they are not. But do not be so certain it's a ruse that you blind yourself to the dangers it might present. Many think that seeing her is a harbinger of tragedy to come," he warned. "And on that note, I have the license. I've spoken with the vicar at the local church, and he's agreed to perform the ceremony tomorrow morning at nine. Mr. Hatton and the vicar's wife will act as witnesses. If you have no objections, of course?"

"No. I have no objections."

Douglas nodded. "Mr. Hatton will meet with you later today to discuss the terms of our arrangement and the support that will be afforded to you once you leave Rosehaven." And imagining that she would leave Rosehaven in a year, that for an entire year, he would face the temptation of her daily—both of those things were a source of unease. "I shall see you at dinner, Miss Jones. Do not wander too far. The ground is uneven, and the rain has left pockets of mud that are quite treacherous."

⋙⋘

LOUISA WATCHED HIM walk away, leaving her standing in the middle of the lane. Alone. And as puzzled as ever. This man who was to be her husband was a mystery to her—a puzzle that demanded solving.

"My own curiosity will be the very death of me," she murmured. But even as she continued her exploration of the gardens and the surrounding grounds, she was mindful of his warning.

When she reached the back of the house, where the formal and decorative gardens gave way to the more functional herb and vegetable gardens of the kitchens, she caught sight of a maid sneaking a rest. Leaning against the side of the house, well away from the windows and the prying eyes of a strict housekeeper or cook, the girl's face paled when she caught sight of Louisa. But Louisa offered a reassuring smile to the young woman. Instantly, the girl's expression changed. It became closed, guarded—perhaps even hostile.

They all knew, Louisa realized. Everyone in the house would know what sort of marriage she had entered into. *That she was not there to stay.* And that meant she would have little authority there. He, her betrothed, couldn't possibly understand the dynamics at play. But she'd known there would be problems of that sort. The servants would not respect her. In truth, she wondered if she would still be able to respect herself.

She was one of them—one of the serving class, and she'd dared to rise above her station, but not for any reason so noble as love. It was a mercenary agreement, and they would all know. The next year would be interesting, indeed.

Retreating to the house once more, she made her way to her chamber. She would wait there until her meeting with Mr. Hatton. But eventually, she knew the issue would have to be addressed.

Chapter Four

"It's too much. I couldn't possibly accept such a generous settlement," Louisa protested. The amount of funds that Mr. Hatton had named was more than she could even imagine. The number was positively astronomical.

"Miss Jones, Mr. Blackwell is aware that you are sacrificing a great deal to enter into this . . . arrangement with him. Trust me when I say that he has considered the settlement he offered very carefully and has reached a more than reasonable figure," Mr. Hatton offered in a placating tone. "Take the offer, Miss Jones. Accept it. You may renegotiate the terms with Mr. Blackwell at the time you part—if you still feel that you need to do so."

Need to part or renegotiate? Hatton's meaning was not clear, and she had the impression that it was intentional. Surely the thin, bespectacled little man was not attempting to play matchmaker! But if he was, if he had some vision of there being a happily ever after for them, he was at least an ally. And she needed one.

"There is one thing, Mr. Hatton . . . the servants."

"Yes, Miss Jones."

"This is an unusual marriage, and regardless of any attempts to keep our private business just that, they will know. And they will gossip. Among themselves or with people outside this house. Those sorts of rumors could be quite damning."

He frowned. "Indeed. You are quite right. I've heard veiled statements already."

"I need to have authority over the household staff. Complete authority so long as I live here."

Mr. Hatton nodded. "I had not considered that your position here would be complicated by your former status as a . . . a. . . ."

"Servant? Yes, while I held an elevated position within the households where I worked, I was still an employee. But those positions are never easy, Mr. Hatton, as you know. You cannot sit with the servants around their dinner table, but you are not always welcome in the family dining room. We are very much trapped between worlds. They will not accept me easily."

Hatton nodded. "Indeed, we are, Miss Jones, and you are quite right. His lordship may not be aware of the difficult position you will be in while residing here, but upon reflection, I can certainly understand it. It might be a situation best handled not by Mr. Blackwell at all but by Miss Mary. You have yet to meet her, but I think it is high time."

In truth, she'd all but forgotten about the doddy aunt. The very reason she had agreed to come to Rosehaven, and the woman had slipped her mind entirely. Louisa flushed. "Certainly, Mr. Hatton."

"No fear, Miss Jones. Show her no fear. She is a bit like an animal. If she senses that she has the upper hand, she will use it."

With that warning echoing in her mind, Mr. Hatton rose and rang the bell pull. Within seconds, a maid entered the room. "Miss Jones wishes an audience with Miss Mary."

The maid's only immediate response was to blink rapidly in shock. Then she composed herself. "I will see when the mistress is available."

"You mistake my meaning, girl," Mr. Hatton stated flatly. "Miss Jones will see Miss Mary. Your task is to inform Miss Mary that she should attend us in the drawing room."

When the maid was gone, Louisa immediately scolded the man.

"Mr. Hatton! I cannot believe you would be so high-handed." Of course, he had arranged her presence there through nothing less than subterfuge and manipulation. Was it truly a surprise? "She will be predisposed to dislike me now."

"My dear girl, she dislikes everyone," he warned. "Trust me when I say that it is best to seize the higher ground and to do so immediately. Strategy is vital."

It was perhaps ten minutes, but no more, when the drawing room door opened once more and an elderly woman entered draped in a gown that was at least three decades out of date. Despite that, it was flattering to her still-slim figure. Her hair might have been blonde in her youth, but it had now turned a perfect snowy white, perhaps aided by powder. She moved with the effortless grace of one much younger. Like a dancer.

Immediately, Louisa thought of the wraith-like figure she'd seen the night before. Was it possible that she had found the very corporeal source of that ghostly vision?

"It is quite impertinent to issue a summons when you are a guest in this house, Miss Jones," the woman intoned disapprovingly.

She was a bit like Mrs. Wheaton, Louisa realized. The woman had wrapped herself in authority to shield herself from the slings and arrows of others. Mr. Hatton's words made much more sense to her in that light. "It was also quite impertinent to have a guest under roof for more than a day without bothering to greet them."

"No quibbling about whether or not you are a guest?" Miss Mary asked. "You came here thinking to be employed and find yourself prepared to take up the role of chatelaine."

"You are correct. I am not a guest, at all. I am betrothed to your nephew and will become mistress of Rosehaven tomorrow," Louisa replied. "But I would not have enmity between us. I understand that it is your position. This house has been your domain—"

"For too bloody long," the woman snapped. "It's about time

someone else saw to the running of this place. It's exhausting, Miss Jones. I will be happy to turn those reins over to you."

Her tone would have shocked some gently bred young lady. But Louisa had grown up in the rookeries, after all, where fishwives shouted and prostitutes called out their wares with equal profanity and enthusiasm. "In that case, I should think you would have been eager to welcome me here."

Miss Mary's chin lifted, and she eyed Louisa with something that might have been approval. "Leave us, Hatton. I can't abide your hovering. I promise not to gobble the girl up. After all, she'll be easing my burdens significantly."

When they were alone, Louisa braced herself for what was to come. It could be anything. The woman was impossible to predict. But Miss Mary did not begin castigating her for her impertinence. Instead, she walked over to Louisa and simply picked up her hand. She turned it palm side up and began to examine it with great interest.

"You've had an interesting life, Miss Jones," Miss Mary observed, delicately tracing lines on Louisa's palm. "This is your life line. For most people, it will fork once. Yours has forked twice. Based on where these forks present along the line, that represents a significant change—once when you were a child and once as an adult. Then it remains strong and steady. What do you think that means?"

"I could not begin to guess, ma'am," Louisa answered. "I've never given much credence to palm reading or any other sort of divination. Being an observant person with a basic understanding of human nature allows those who would call themselves soothsayers to feed people what they want to hear."

Miss Mary's head lifted, her chin jutting forward in challenge. "And for those of us who do not care what they want to hear?"

"I meant no offense. But I prefer to put my faith in more rational things," Louisa insisted.

Miss Mary dropped her hand. "You will humor me, Miss Jones.

Come to the table here, by the window."

Louisa rose, following Miss Mary to the spot she had indicated. From a pocket concealed within the folds of her skirt, the older women withdrew a deck of cards. Tarot. Louisa had seen them before, used by a fortune teller at a fair. She put no faith in such things, but if humoring Miss Mary would ease her way at Rosehaven, she'd tolerate it.

"Choose three cards," Miss Mary instructed.

Louisa did as she was bid. Miss Mary spread those cards in a line and then turned over seven more cards, forming a cross with them. For the longest moment, she simply stared at the cards, studying them one by one, then drawing back to take in the full array.

"There is darkness ahead of you," Miss Mary said, her voice laced with warning. "But not without hope. You have the strength to overcome it . . . but do you have the will?"

It was nonsense. Vague statements that could be interpreted in dozens of ways depending upon what she wanted to believe. Louisa tapped her finger on one of those cards. "What does this card mean?"

Miss Mary smiled much like the cat who'd gotten the cream. "That would be the lovers, Miss Jones."

If she'd needed proof that Miss Mary's reading was nonsense, that did it. Mr. Blackwell wanted nothing to do with her, at least not for very long.

"Do you know why Mr. Blackwell wishes to marry me?"

Miss Mary shrugged. "I know why he refused you at first. You are too pretty, Miss Jones, for a man like my nephew to resist."

"A man like your nephew?"

"One who struggles with his inner nature, one who fights to find balance between passion and reason. You tempt him, and that is what he seeks to avoid at all costs. But time is running out, and now he has to play the hand that fate—and Mr. Hatton—have dealt him."

"You are mistaken, madame!"

Miss Mary tapped one long, elegant finger against the card in question. *The Lovers.* "Not I, Miss Jones. I merely relay what the cards tell me. But even when fate sends us down one path, we must choose whether to stay on it or change course. You will find your own way. And perhaps he will too. I will see you at dinner, Miss Jones. And felicitations on your pending nuptials."

"Thank you, ma'am."

"Good afternoon, Miss Jones—Louisa. I shall call you Louisa. Too much of this Miss Jones and Miss Mary and ma'am business. I will be Aunt Mary to you," the woman declared. "After tomorrow, of course."

And with that, she breezed from the drawing room, leaving Louisa shaken. Like one might be in the wake of a powerful storm.

Chapter Five

IT WAS A shockingly brief and perfunctory service. There was no celebratory breakfast awaiting them when they returned to Rosehaven. In truth, hardly a word was spoken in the carriage on the way home.

Douglas spared a glance at Miss Jones—Mrs. Louisa Blackwell, he corrected—and noted the tension that had settled over her pretty features. He wanted to dispel it, to offer some assurance that they hadn't just made a terrible mistake. But how could he? For him, it had been the right choice. The only choice. But for her, she'd given up any hope of having a family of her own. The twinge of guilt that thought created within him was decidedly uncomfortable.

Of course, stealing glances at her had other unfortunate effects. She was alluring. In a way that was completely effortless, she commanded his attention. How many times during the previous day had he halted what he was doing when thoughts of her and their situation intruded? Countless, he admitted. Proximity only made his growing obsession with her more evident. It also underscored his decision to keep their relationship as brief as his uncle's will would allow. He could not afford to indulge his preoccupation with her. *She could not afford for him to do so.* One year, and he would watch her walk out of his life forever. If he'd endured the hell of various wars for nearly a decade, surely he could achieve that.

Douglas hadn't told her the entire truth. Certainly, he did like an orderly life, and emotional upheaval was something he had worked very hard to avoid. But he hadn't told her why. He hadn't dared to disclose to her the terrible fate that so many women met when they had the misfortune to become entangled with a Blackwell man. Jealous. Possessive. Irrational. Whether it was love or something much darker, Blackwell men could not be trusted when it came to the safety of the women in their lives.

When the carriage finally drew to a stop, he breathed a sigh of relief. He needed distance between them—a reprieve from his own thoughts. But luck was not on his side. The moment he stepped down from the carriage, he heard the sound of hoofbeats. A lone rider was coming up the drive.

It was all Douglas could do not to curse bitterly. As if, he thought, there weren't enough complications in his life already, his cousin had arrived.

"Ho, Douglas! Felicitations," Terrence Blackwell called out as he halted his horse. With one graceful motion, he dismounted, his booted feet crunching on the gravel. "I've arrived just in time to celebrate your nuptials."

The words rang hollowly, no doubt as they'd been intended to. His marriage to Louisa meant that Terrence was no longer the contingent heir. Had Douglas failed to meet his late uncle's conditions in the time allotted, the family fortune would have been Terrence's for the taking, so long as he managed to get himself married. It could not be coincidence that he had showed up now.

"Terrence," Douglas acknowledged. "I wasn't aware you'd planned to visit."

His cousin's answering smile did not reach his eyes. His gaze remained cold and sharp. "I wasn't aware that I had to inform you, cousin. It is the family home, after all. You are merely its caretaker for this generation. Isn't that how Uncle James stated it in his will?"

It was, and now he was trapped by his uncle's last wishes. "Of course, Terrence. We will have the servants ready your usual room."

"And in the meantime, you may introduce me to your charming bride."

Douglas gritted his teeth. "Of course." Turning back to the carriage, he caught the worried gaze of his bride. She stared at him with concern. *As if she knew something was amiss.* Forcing himself to offer a reassuring smile, he offered her his hand and helped her alight from the vehicle. "Louisa, allow me to introduce my cousin, Mr. Terrence Blackwell. Terrence, my wife, Louisa."

Terrence stepped forward, taking her hand and bowing low over it before pressing a kiss to it. "It is an honor to meet you, Cousin Louisa."

"Likewise, Mr. Blackwell," she murmured softly.

Douglas found himself watching her closely, gauging her reaction. Terrence was handsome and charming. He had no qualms about seducing married women. And he didn't seem overly concerned about the family curse and what it might do to any woman he entangled himself with. But Louisa seemed immune to his charm. She didn't blush or stammer in his presence. Instead she leveled an assessing stare at him and kept close to Douglas's side. He should not have been grateful for that, but he was. "Let us adjourn inside and enjoy some refreshment. I do believe a storm is coming in."

LOUISA TRIED TO contain her shudder. Terrence Blackwell was not a man to be trusted. Based on the tension she could feel emanating from her husband, he was well aware of the fact. What was the source of the enmity between them? Did it have something to do with the inheritance that had prompted their marriage? And, if so, did that mean Terrence also posed a threat to her? She had far more questions than answers, but it had been that way since her arrival at Rosehaven.

Ill at ease, she placed her hand on Douglas's arm and allowed him to lead her into the house. Douglas. Only the day before, he'd been Mr. Blackwell. The day before that, he'd been a complete stranger. Then Louisa realized she'd have to write to Effie. She would be expecting word, and if she didn't receive it, the Duchess of Clarenden would descend upon them in her very impressive fury.

The butler, with cool disapproval apparent in his tone, informed them that a meal of cold meats and cheese had been laid in the breakfast room for them. Miss Mary was awaiting them there.

"Did you stay in the village last night?" Douglas asked his cousin.

"No, I'm just down from London this morning. Left at first light and rode hard all the way," Terrence replied.

Lies. Louisa didn't even need her intuition to know that. His horse had been fresh and rested when he arrived. There was no way that horse had been ridden all the way from London just that morning. A glance at her husband, who was facing away from his cousin, showed that his jaw hardened considerably, tension and anger transforming his features. He knew. He knew that Terrence was lying. But what a thing to lie about. What purpose did it serve?

With her hand still on his arm, Louisa squeezed gently. He glanced over at her, but the look that passed between them was one of understanding.

"Terrence, what in heaven's name are you doing here?" Aunt Mary asked. "After the last time, I would have thought you too ashamed to show your face here. I certainly would have been."

Louisa glanced over her shoulder at Terrence. There was an almost imperceptible tightening of his features and a hardness in his gaze, but the cool smile never left his face.

"I've always had a quick temper, Aunt Mary," the man answered. "It was a shock, of course, to discover the terms of Uncle James's will and how I'd essentially been all but disinherited unless Douglas failed to do as he'd been told. But then, Douglas always does what he is told, doesn't he?"

There was no disguising the bitterness that infused his words. But then he continued, "Alas, I wouldn't be here if I could be in London. I've gotten into a bit of a bind with one of the gaming halls, scoundrel that I am. I'll not be able to show my face in London until the next annuity from the estate is deposited."

Not a lie, Louisa decided, but most definitely a half truth.

"Well, it is the family home, and to our eternal dismay, you are family," Aunt Mary conceded.

The animosity between everyone in that room was palpable. It was exhausting. "I find I'm not very hungry, but with the excitement of the day, I am a bit tired. I think I'll lie down for a bit."

"Let me show you to your new room," Douglas offered.

New room? She'd be moving into the master suite with her husband. While theirs wasn't to be a lasting marriage, it was to be a real one for the duration of the year.

"Thank you, I confess to still being a bit lost here," she replied with a smile that belied her nerves. Then they exited the room, leaving Mary and Terrence to verbally swipe at one another.

Chapter Six

As they entered the master suite, Douglas was furious. He'd wanted distance between them. He'd wanted to ensure that he was as far from temptation as possible. Yes, their marriage would have been consummated regardless, but they were practically strangers. It had never been his intent to pounce on her the very day of their wedding without the benefit of knowing one another better. But Terrence's arrival had changed everything in an instant. Louisa would no longer be in her chamber down the hall until she was comfortable, but moved into the master suite with him until such time as Terrence left. And given what he'd said about not being able to return to London, that would not be for some time.

"I'm sorry," he said. "I hadn't intended that we should share these chambers . . . yet."

"I'm aware. I'm also very aware of why the plans must change. Your cousin is not to be trusted."

He laughed bitterly. "You have no idea just how true that is. He is dangerous, Louisa. Whatever you do, do not let yourself be caught alone with him."

She laughed, the musical sound slightly tinged with bitterness. "You do not know the full extent of my upbringing, sir."

"Douglas. We are married. Addressing me so formally might raise questions that we do not want to answer."

She nodded. "Douglas. You are quite right. But to allay your fears, I spent the earliest years of my life in St. Giles. My mother and I shared a room with another woman, her husband, and their two children. It was relatively warm and dry, but far from safe. I know only too well when a man has nefarious intentions. You develop a sense for those things after a while."

Douglas couldn't fathom that the delicately pretty creature before him, with her soft features and ivory skin, had not just come from such a place but managed to survive it by her wits. The realities of life in the rookeries—squalid, impoverished, crime- and disease-ridden—were beyond harsh.

"I am sorry you had to go through that," he offered, uncertain what else to say.

Her lips quirked. "I am not. Everything that I have experienced in life has shaped me into the person I am today. I am rather happy with who I am. Would you alter the course of your past if it meant being someone different from who you are today?"

"I do not know, truthfully. Regardless, we need to discuss our current situation and how it has altered the way we might deal with one another."

"You wish for me to stay here in the master suite with you," she surmised. "There are two bedchambers?"

"There are," he said. "But I do not think that will be sufficient for our plan to work. The servants here have no loyalty to me. I have been away for many, many years. Most of them had never laid eyes upon me until this past year when my uncle died. But Terrence grew up here and lived here off and on for the decade I was with the army. He has their fealty."

He saw her uncertainty. Her expression shifted almost imperceptibly before she once more schooled it into impassivity. "Then we are to share a bed chamber?"

"Yes. Until he leaves, which may not be for some time. Months, perhaps," he admitted. "I had thought that we might take our time and get to know one another a bit before we embarked on the more intimate part of our marriage—to give you some distance and privacy as we adjust to this new state."

"To be perfectly clear, the distance and privacy were entirely your idea. Not mine. I understood when I agreed to the marriage what I was committing myself to."

It was as if all the air had been sucked from the room. God above! The more he discovered about her, the more fascinating he found her.

She cocked her head to one side, staring at him curiously. "How well must we know one another for it to be enough?"

⋙⋘

HE'D STEPPED CLOSER to her with each word, until they stood toe to toe. Staring up into his dark gaze, Louisa felt herself swaying toward him. She'd never been kissed. But growing up as she did, she certainly knew more about it than many young ladies did. And all the nonsense from Alexandra's gothic novels made it sound positively divine. "How well do you normally know the women you take to your bed?"

The moment the question escaped her lips, she wished she could call it back. It was terribly provocative. And bold. So very, very bold.

His lips curved in a smirk. "There is no way to answer that question that does not cast me in a negative light. I think it's best, always, to let the woman in question decide what is well enough. But perhaps there is a small experiment we might try."

"Oh? And what is that?" she asked. Was that truly her? There was no denying the flirtatious challenge in her voice, but where in heaven's name had it come from?

"A kiss, Louisa. Only a kiss."

Before she could think of some appropriate response, he'd simply swooped in. His lips covered hers, moving over them in a way that was mesmerizing. For all his seeming indifference to her initially, that kiss was a revelation. It was gentle but insistent. Generous and also demanding. It was not at all what she had thought. She'd certainly seen others kissing and so much more. But she'd never experienced it. She'd never known that it would sweep her away into a haze of pleasure.

When his arms closed about her, pulling her against him, her lips parted in surprise. He swiftly took advantage and deepened the kiss. And Louisa was simply lost to it. All thought fled and she clung to him, ready for whatever might come next.

Chapter Seven

DOUGLAS PUNCTUATED THAT kiss with a slight nip, his teeth scraping gently over the lushness of her lower lip. The shiver it elicited from her was enough to test his resolve. He wasn't going to bed her. Not yet. Despite the intense desire he felt for her and her apparent willingness, he knew that wasn't quite enough. Louisa, with her sweet and passionate response, was still an innocent. And they had known one another only three days. He was selfish enough to want it, but not self-serving enough to give in to those desires.

Forcing himself to gentle the kiss, to ease it back from the cusp of calamity and to something sweeter, something that was far more about romance than about naked lust. When his breathing had slowed, when the blood that had been racing in his veins returned to its normal pace, he pulled back more still. With a final brush of his lips against hers, he released her.

"That was not how I intended for things to go. I want to be certain that when you invite me to your bed, Louisa, it's because you want me there and not because you feel it is simply what a wife is supposed to do. We have enough things stacked against us in this without adding the weight of obligation."

She shook her head. "You are mistaken, Douglas. Nothing that has passed between us has been because I felt it was what I ought to do. If I were concerned with that, I would have refused you outright."

The startled laugh that erupted from him shocked them both. It had been a long while since he had laughed. Certainly, he hadn't since returning to Rosehaven. "Indeed. I suppose you would have. In light of that, Louisa, I would advise you to rest while you may. I imagine there will not be any sleep for you tonight."

"Where are you going then?"

All trace of amusement fled. "To find out precisely what Terrence is doing here and what he really wants. Nothing he says can ever be taken at face value."

With that resolve firm in his mind, he turned and left the room. It was best that she not be present for his confrontation with Terrence. She was a distraction for him, and with his cousin, having all of one's faculties about was imperative.

He found him in the billiard room. It was where Terrence normally spent the majority of his time while in residence. Or at least, it always had been. It seemed his habits had not changed.

"Cousin, I would have thought you had better things to do today than keep me company," Terrence said, lifting his gaze from the billiard table even as he took his shot.

Douglas nodded in agreement. "Certainly more enjoyable things, but then there is little that would not be preferable to being in your company. I cannot simply toss you out of this house, not without providing other suitable lodgings for you. Uncle James made that a contingency, didn't he? Now I must support you regardless of whatever wastrel endeavors you throw yourself into."

Terrence lined up the next shot. "Unless your marriage is dissolved. Or something happens to either of you before the year is out. . . . What a pity that would be."

As the billiard ball sailed down its path, Douglas slammed his hand down on the table, sending the shot awry. "Do not threaten her . . . or me. You will regret it, Terrence. I'm not the easy-tempered boy you remember. And I know now what you are capable of. Stay away from

Louisa. Hide out here from your creditors as you like, but make no mistake that I will hand you over to them myself if you make too much of a nuisance of yourself."

Douglas didn't wait for his cousin to reply. Instead, he turned on his heel and walked out. Behind him, he heard the crashing and banging indicative of Terrence's temper tantrum. He didn't smile. There was no satisfaction in it. Terrence was dangerous, but for the time being, his hands were tied. Unless he provided other suitable lodgings for Terrence, he was forced to let him remain at Rosehaven.

"So I'll find him suitable accommodations," he murmured and detoured to the library. He'd have Hatton look into the matter. The man knew the contents of his late uncle's will front to back. If there was a way around it, he would know.

LOUISA HAD RETREATED to a small settee in the sitting room of the master suite. It hadn't been her intent to fall asleep, but the nerves of the day, the restlessness from the night before, and the strange mix of emotions which had resulted from the kiss she'd shared with Douglas that morning had left her overwhelmed. Sleep had been a reprieve from the turmoil.

But she awoke with a shiver. The room around her was freezing. A fact that should have been impossible. It was the tail end of August, after all. Even as dismal as English weather could often be, an icy chill to the air defied all explanation.

Unable to simply shrug it off as her imagination, Louisa did something that would have made Alexandra proud even as she cringed. "What do you want? I know you are here. I can feel your presence!"

The answer came in the form of a loud thump near the door—as if someone had banged on the wall. Louisa was terrified, though she knew it would not be to her benefit to let that be known. So she rose and walked towards the spot where the noise had originated from. No sooner had she reached it than the doorknob rattled. It was a clear indication that she should follow whatever it was to wherever it might lead.

Three times, Louisa thought. Three times, whatever that presence was, it had reached out to her in some way. It had caused her no harm beyond raising a bit of gooseflesh on her skin. Even as she told herself that, her heart was racing. It beat in her chest like a drum as she opened the door and stepped out into the corridor.

Looking left to right, she waited for some sort of sign. It came with the fluttering of a curtain at the opposite end of the hall. With a mix of false bravado, reluctant courage, and curiosity, she headed in that direction.

It was almost like a child's game, being led about by knocks, bangs and ruffled drapery. Was it the spirit of a child? She dearly hoped not. Perhaps it was the only way the spirit had to communicate with the living. The particulars of how that all worked was something of a mystery to her. No doubt Alexandra would have known instantly.

"I should have paid more attention to those horrid novels," Louisa murmured.

When she'd turned at the end of the corridor into another wing of the house, she simply stopped and waited. This time, it was a plume of dust which led her to a door near the end. Reaching for the handle, she was somewhat surprised when it turned easily beneath her hand. And yet, when she pushed the door, it did not open easily. The wood had swollen with the heat and humidity. She was forced to put her hip against the door and shove with all her might.

When it finally crashed inward, she stumbled into the musty room. The curtains were drawn tightly. Only a small sliver of light managed to penetrate. It was enough that she could see the outline of furniture dropped in holland cloth. Stepping deeper into the room, she narrowly skirted a settee at the foot of the bed to reach the window.

Pulling the curtains wide, she secured them and then turned to take a better look.

It was a room very similar to the one she'd been given on her arrival, at least in terms of size. Tugging one of the dusty furniture coverings away, she found rich, rosewood pieces inlaid with delicate patterns. There was something about the room itself that felt *feminine*. Whomever that room had belonged to had been a woman. Of that much she was certain.

Curious but also compelled, she moved to one of the pieces of furniture hidden beneath its dusty shroud. Tugging the fabric away, she found herself staring at a small writing table. The curious thing was that it appeared to have been left in a state as if the person who had been using it might walk in at any moment. There was a half-written letter lying atop it and a quill dipped in ink that had been dried for years.

Picking up the elegant stationery, Louisa instantly felt uncomfortable. As if it were a terrible violation of privacy . . . because the letter was addressed to her husband.

My dearest Douglas,

I am a horrid creature for hoping this letter does not find you well at all. I hope it finds you in the same agonizing misery that I currently contend with—the loneliness I feel when we are not together. The days without you seem to grow longer each time you return to university.

When I think of how you urged me to run away with you, to elope, I find myself regretting my refusal. Even though I know it was the right thing to do, that you must finish your education and that we must marry in a respectable manner, I cannot help wishing the days until that may happen had already passed. What I would not give to know that at your next visit home we would be married, instead of merely enjoying another all-too-brief holiday together.
Your uncle

And that was where the letter stopped. No signature. No indication of the author's identity. Only of her expectation that she would one day occupy the position that Louisa currently held as Mrs. Douglas Blackwell.

It wasn't jealousy that she felt. She certainly was not entitled to feel such a thing. But she did feel deceived in some ways. Should he have told her that he'd been on the cusp of marrying someone else? Someone else who had, if her instincts were correct, met a very tragic end?

"Who are you?" Louisa whispered to the empty room. But it wasn't empty. Not truly. That familiar rush of cold air surrounded her for an instant before receding. As it did, a small compartment beneath the writing desk sprang open—a hidden drawer.

Dropping to her knees, heedless of the dust, she reached into that drawer and brought out a cloth-wrapped bundle. The cloth itself was a lovely cream and blue paisley shawl. Within its folds, she found a small leather-bound book that was obviously a journal and several letters addressed to Miss Caroline Farris. What had become of her? And if it was her, why did her spirit still linger at Rosehaven?

With far more questions than answers circulating in her mind, Louisa elected to take the lot of it with her. Lifting her skirts, she tied the shawl about her waist and created a pocket of sorts. Why she felt the need to conceal those items she did not understand. But if Caroline Farris had felt that they needed to be hidden away, she wasn't going to brandish them about for others to see. She would have answers, and there was only person to ask. It was not her husband.

Chapter Eight

Louisa found Aunt Mary in the morning room. She was drinking her tea and staring intently at the cards spread out before her.

"And whose fortune are you telling now?"

Mary shrugged, lifting one elegant shoulder. "No one in particular. I'm simply seeing what the future in this house may hold."

Louisa stepped deeper into the room. When she reached the table, she looked down at the assortment of cards and felt a shiver race through her. They looked quite ominous. "What is this?"

"The Tower," Mary replied. "It warns of impending chaos and trouble. There are dark times ahead at Rosehaven, my dear. Secrets," she added, tapping another card, "hidden agendas, lies. Dark times, indeed."

"Who was Caroline Farris?"

Louisa couldn't say who was more startled by the question, Mary or herself. She'd intended to ease her way into that conversation, to subtly and slyly conduct her investigation. Clearly, she had failed. She'd changed her gown to one that gave her actual pockets and now removed the journal tucked inside it. The letters, she had hidden in their rooms. They were intimate in a way that she could not imagine Douglas would wish his aunt to be privy to.

"You've been snooping," Mary finally replied, but there was no censure in her voice.

"Not snooping. I was invited."

Mary's eyebrows lifted. "By whom?"

"Caroline Farris," Louisa replied. "Or whatever remains of her in this house."

Mary blinked in surprise. "You've seen her?"

Louisa took the seat opposite her. "Not exactly. I have . . . felt her presence. Cold spots, drafts, a fluttering curtain. And while I would like to dismiss those as simply the vagaries of an old house, we are in the throes of summer heat. And by following those things, she led me to her room and to that journal. The question I have, is why?"

Mary leaned forward, her voice barely above a whisper. "There are ways to find out. There is a woman I know who claims to have the ability to commune with the spirit world. She is in London. I will write to her . . . but are your prepared for the answers, Louisa?"

"I don't know," she admitted. "I must speak with Douglas."

"He's gone out," Mary said. "I saw him riding away earlier this morning. He appeared to be in quite a temper. Likely because of his conversation with Terrence. That boy does certainly know how to get under everyone's skin."

"Man. He's not a boy at all, is he? He's a man fully grown and should have the corresponding accountability for his actions. To call him a boy is to facilitate his continued immaturity."

Mary blinked in surprise. Then she laughed. "I like you, Louisa. I do not say that about many people. But I do like you. It's the rare bird who isn't afraid to speak her mind so freely. Are you intimidated by anything at all?"

"I haven't encountered it yet. I'm certain it exists, however. I think I'll go back upstairs. When Douglas returns, will you tell him I'd like to speak with him?"

With Mary's nod of agreement, Louisa left the drawing room and made her way back upstairs. Once again, she was left only with more questions. What had happened between Douglas and Terrence to invoke his temper?

As she reached the top of the stairs, she saw the same maid she'd seen once before—the one who'd been loitering outside the kitchen. Once again, she was not working. But this wasn't simply shirking her duties. The girl was giggling in Terrence's arms as he kissed her neck. It was clear that they were well and intimately acquainted with one another.

"What is the meaning of this?"

Terrence pulled himself away from the maid long enough to give her a scathing look, before dismissively adding, "You are a married woman. If it requires explanation, my cousin is more of a prig than I thought." With that, the two disappeared into one of the many bedrooms along the corridor, their laughter echoing behind them.

Impotently furious, Louisa lifted her chin and made her way back to the master suite. The insolence and utter disregard for propriety was bad enough, but there was something even more disturbing about it. There had been a familiarity between Terrence and the maid, Fanny, who, according to what Louisa had discovered earlier, had only been employed at Rosehaven for a few months. And Terrence, allegedly, hadn't been back to Rosehaven since the reading of James Blackwell's will. So when had there even been an opportunity for them to meet?

IT WAS LATE when Douglas arrived home. His earlier encounter with Terrence had already put him in a foul mood, but his meeting with Hatton had only worsened it. Unless Terrence did something truly diabolical, they were stuck. The will had stated that Terrence could only be denied the right to reside at Rosehaven if he posed a threat to its other inhabitants or until he was no longer the heir apparent to its current owner.

So he might have a child with Louisa, something he had not planned to do at all. Or wait for Terrence to actually bring harm to someone. Those were his options. Neither was acceptable. The first for a variety of reasons and the length of time that would be required. The second because it was the very thing he hoped to avoid.

Passing the butler in the entryway, he directed, "Have a tray sent up for Mrs. Blackwell and myself. We will dine in our suite tonight."

"Certainly, sir," the elderly man replied with a note of censure in his voice. It was clear that he held Louisa in some disregard.

"Let me make something very clear. My wife will run this household to her satisfaction. If she says a staff member should be fired, they will be fired. If she says she dislikes the way someone is fulfilling their duties, then her word is law, and they will be sent packing. I've tolerated your rudeness and disrespect for long enough. I will not have her tolerate it, as well. And if that is a problem for you, you may collect your severance and leave immediately."

The aged servant ducked his head in his first ever display of deference. "Certainly, sir. I shall be certain that all the staff is made aware of Mrs. Blackwell's authority."

Taking the stairs, Douglas made his way directly to the master suite. When he entered, Louisa was seated at a small table. Spread out before her was a small book and several letters. But she wasn't looking at them. She was looking at him and had clearly been waiting for some time.

It was bad form to abandon one's wife on their wedding day, regardless of the circumstances of their marriage. "I'm sorry. I had to get out for a while. I wasn't fit company for anyone. Discovering that we are likely stuck with Terrence for the duration put me in a foul mood."

"Well, I'm on the verge of making it much worse, I'm afraid. But first, tell me about Caroline Farris."

The last thing he'd expected was to hear that name from Louisa. In truth, he rarely spoke of Caroline to anyone. "She was my uncle's ward. We grew up here together."

"And you were in love," she said. There was no accusation in her voice. It was merely an observation.

He considered his answer carefully. "I thought I was, but we were very young. So young that I think neither of us was capable of really loving someone. Had she lived, we would have married, and we might have been happy together . . . but I do not know. I'm not certain anyone who is a member of this family is capable of love."

"How did she die?"

A sigh escaped him. He didn't talk about Caroline—hadn't even spoken her name in years. "She had a riding accident. There was nothing she loved better than her horses, and she was the most accomplished equestrienne I have ever seen. But even the most skilled rider can have an accident. She was thrown and struck her head on a stone. When we found her, she was unconscious. And when we brought her home, she lingered in that state for several days, before ultimately passing away."

"I do not think it was an accident. I think she was murdered . . . and her spirit is lingering here at Rosehaven."

Chapter Nine

LOUISA WATCHED HIM react to her statement. Denial, disbelief, anger. She saw all of those things flash by. That they knew one another so little and still she could read him so clearly was both strange and comforting.

At last, he demanded of her, "Why would you say such a thing?"

Louisa took a deep breath and prepared to tell him the strange truth. "All of my life, I've had a certain instinctive understanding of when I am in danger . . . and of who is dangerous. I've trusted those instincts, and that have never steered me wrong. The first day that I was here, when you left me in the library, I felt this strange chill. The air wasn't just cold, but it moved and undulated. Surrounding me. And while I was startled, I didn't feel threatened."

"That is hardly proof," he said skeptically.

"It happened again that night in my room, when I saw the figure in white."

"Then what you saw could not have been Caroline—"

"No," she concurred. "It was not. What I saw was a living, breathing person with actual form. Of that, I am entirely certain. And I have a suspicion of who that person was. But first, I need to tell you about my encounter with Caroline today."

That was greeted with stony silence. Then after a moment, a curt nod. It was clear that he was far from convinced. Still, Louisa continued. "I did have a bit of a nap this morning. When I awakened, it was to that same strange cold sensation. The window was open, but it's terribly hot outside. There is not even a hint of a breeze. And yet that cold air was whirling about me. And I decided that there must be a reason for it. So I told this spirit to lead me to what it wanted. And it did."

"How?"

"First was a thump on the wall beside the door. Then the curtains stirred at the end of the hall. I took that turn. Then outside what I assume had been Caroline's room, a puff of dust came from beneath the door... perfectly silhouetted against the light so that I might see it."

"Again, that is not proof."

"No. But of all the rooms in this house for me to wander into, isn't it strange that the one I discovered was hers? And that while I was in that room, the secret drawer beneath the writing table simply sprang open and revealed all that you see here . . . her journal, the letters that the two of you exchanged."

"So you think Caroline's ghost has contacted you because she's jealous?"

Louisa shook her head. "Not at all. I think she's reaching out because she thinks I am in danger . . . the same sort of danger she was in, because Terrence was the one who killed her."

Silence filled the small room. He didn't say a word. Louisa kept waiting for him to have some explosion of temper, or worse, to simply laugh in her face. But ultimately, she decided that his silence might be worse. "Say something, for heaven's sake," she admonished after it became intolerable.

"That is quite a leap. You spent a great deal of your formative years surrounded by those with criminal intent, and it has colored your perception of the world. What reason would Terrence have to kill Caroline?"

Louisa spread her hands. "To prevent you marrying her and having an heir. Had you married your uncle's ward, there is little question that the outcome of your uncle's will would not have changed, even if the contingencies within it did. The fortune would have been yours, and he would have nothing. And now, because we have married, he is at risk of losing everything once more. Do you think it a coincidence that he showed up here on the same day we married? That he stood there next to his fresh, well-rested horse and told us he'd ridden all the way from London just this morning? If I spent too much time around the criminally intended, Douglas, you have spent too little."

HE WANTED TO deny all of it. Not because it was unbelievable, but because it was entirely believable. Not wanting a thing to be true did not make it so. If he'd stayed there, married Caroline when they were younger and not left to join the army, would she have still been alive? Had Terrence really killed her? He wished that he could so easily deny the claim, but he had little doubt his cousin was capable of such a thing. The question was whether or not there had been opportunity.

"What have you gleaned from reading her letters and journals?" There was a bite to his tone, one that he could not help. It felt like an invasion of privacy, but then, they were now married and privacy was very much a thing of the past. How could he resent it if what she said was true? He'd never encountered a ghost or apparition. At least, he hadn't to his knowledge, but he couldn't outright deny that such things existed when his uncle had been such a firm believer. Indeed, the entirety of Pluckley believed it. And if ever there was a rational source for such accounts, surely it would be Louisa Blackwell nee Jones.

"I haven't read them. I did read the half-finished letter that she'd been in the middle of writing to you. When I realized who the letters were intended for and who they had likely come from, I felt it wasn't my place to read them. I have looked at her journal a bit, but only to flip through it until I could find the last entries . . . the events leading up to her death."

"They were fairly innocent," he admitted. Then wryly added, "But not entirely."

"We are not in love. We were not married or betrothed at that time. Our worlds·were completely separate, and our paths had never crossed. There is no betrayal in this, and there is no jealousy. You had a life before we met. Likely one that involved more women than simply Caroline Farris. And I daresay when our year is up, there will be women after we part ways," she offered with a very matter-of-fact shrug.

It irked him—the notion that she was completely unbothered by the idea of him with another. And while it had been his wish to live apart, he wanted her to be at least somewhat aggrieved by the fact. "Indeed. You are remarkably rational about these matters, and that is why I find your account of your interactions with this *spirit* to be credible. But I would hope that it is not Caroline. I would hope that she has found peace."

"Perhaps this is why she is not yet at peace," she suggested. "If we can uncover the truth of the events surrounding her death, it might ease her soul."

Moving towards the table where she sat, he took the chair next to her and began perusing the assorted letters. Most of them were innocent. A few of them hinted at the passionate kisses he had shared with Caroline. But mindful of how innocent she had been, things between them had never progressed beyond that.

He had often written back to Caroline on the same stationery she had sent to him, turning it sideways and writing overtop of and in between her large, flowery scrawl. It seemed as though a century had passed between that time and the present. He certainly felt a century older.

"What children we were," he mused.

Louisa opened the journal, turning it to the last entry and passing it to him. "That is the most damning entry."

Picking it up, he scanned the entry. And his blood ran cold.

Loathsome Terrence has come home. No doubt he's heard that Douglas and I intend to marry when he returns from London next week. He's here to pester poor Uncle James about his share of the estate. If he were left all the money in England, he would manage to spend every last drop. 'Tis simply his way.

I've taken to avoiding him. I eat my meals in my room. I spend as much time as possible away from the house. I go riding. I take baskets of food to the poorest of the tenant families. Most of them will not accept it because it comes from Rosehaven. Superstitious nonsense, really. I've looked for the lady in white countless times and have yet to see her. It's likely one of the baker's shameless daughters sneaking about to meet a footman . . . or Terrence.

How I hope that Uncle James will give him enough money that he will once more go back to London and leave us here in peace. His presence disrupts the entire household.

The entry was dated three days before the fateful ride that had ended in Caroline's tragic fall. Six days before she died. And he hadn't realized that Terrence had been there the entire time. His cousin had told him that he'd arrived only shortly before he himself had, and he'd taken him at his word. He had been too distraught to do anything else.

"I should have been here," he said. "If I'd been here, she would not have felt the need to hide from Terrence. She would not have been without someone to protect her from him."

She shook her head. "For what it is worth, he would have simply found another way. He wanted to ensure that you were on equal bachelor footing when your uncle died. That was the only way he could be certain that the will wouldn't be changed, and he would have had allies in this house then just as he does now. The woman in white that I saw my first night here . . . I believe it was the maid, Fanny. I saw them together in the corridor today. They were very familiar with one another, and not simply in the liberties he was taking. Beyond that, they seemed to be well-known to one another."

He knew the maid she spoke of, and he also knew that the girl had only come to work there six months earlier. The butler had stated she was his niece, though that had always seemed a rather dubious claim. To his knowledge, the man had never acknowledged having any family at all.

"Then we send her packing immediately."

"If we do that," she protested, "then we give up any advantage we have. For the time being, until we know precisely what he's planning, we need to go on as if nothing has been discovered about his past crimes."

"So we just pretend to be lost in newly wedded bliss and oblivious to everything else going on?" he asked.

Louisa's answering blush told him, without her needing to say a word, that she was thinking of the kiss they had shared that morning. It had never been far from his mind. Even when he'd been tending to other things, that awareness of her, of how much that simple kiss had stirred his desire for her, had been ever present.

"I think bliss might be a bit of a stretch. After all, everyone is fully aware of your reasons for marrying me," she replied.

"What the world thinks of us isn't important, Louisa. All that matters, at least for the next twelve months, is how we deal with one another. I want to kiss you again, but only if you want that too."

She was silent for a moment, staring into his eyes. Whatever she saw there must have swayed her, because she simply launched herself into his arms. And he was selfish enough to accept all that she offered.

Chapter Ten

SHE HADN'T MEANT to quite literally throw herself at him. But she couldn't regret it because kissing him felt like a little bit of heaven. When his lips touched hers, she could forget about Terrence and whatever schemes were afoot. She could forget about the ghostly presence at Rosehaven. *She could forget that everything between them was only temporary.*

His arms had closed around her, but his hands were far from still. They moved over her back, her shoulders, her hips. And everywhere he touched her, she burned. The pins fell from her hair, one by one, as he plucked them free. When the mass of it was loose, he buried his hands in it.

But Louisa was not content to be a passive participant. She explored his body as well, marveling at the firmness of his flesh which was so very different from her own. Then he was pulling back from her. Immediately, she missed the heat of that kiss.

"I'm sorry, Louisa. I didn't intend for things to go quite so far," he explained, his voice roughened and his breathing a bit ragged.

"Do you regret that they did?"

"I should," he said. "But I won't lie to you."

"My only regret is that you stopped," she admitted, her voice little more than a whisper. "It is our wedding night, after all."

"You should have time to get to know me—"

"I know all that I need to know. I know that I can trust you. Do not ask me how I know, but I do," she insisted. "And we do not have the luxury of waiting. Terrence would challenge the validity of our marriage in order to claim everything for himself."

"This thing between us has nothing to do with Terrence. His presence is simply a reminder of what else is at stake. But you and I . . . this is only about us, what we feel and what we want." It was uttered firmly, but the doubt was easily visible in his gaze.

"If you think I'm trying to seduce you out of obligation, you are mistaken," Louisa said. "I know what I'm doing. And I know what I want. I'm not some shrinking violet who with no notion of what passes between a husband and wife. So when I say I want this, I know precisely what that means."

Apparently her words convinced him. He rose from the chair, lifting her easily into his arms, before striding toward his bedchamber.

Nerves, excitement, desire. The mix of feelings left her breathless, but none of that swayed her from the feeling that what they were about to do was right. And when he deposited her on the bed, Louisa raised herself up on her elbows and watched as he began stripping off his clothes. His coat and cravat were first, followed by his waistcoat and shirt.

It was a marvel to look at him. Smooth, sun-bronzed skin over firm, sculpted muscle. The dark hair covering his chest and bisecting his ridged abdomen tempted her. She wanted to touch him, to feel that beneath her fingertips. So she did. She sat up and reached for him, her fingers trailing over his skin to appease her curiosity.

But he gripped her wrist, halting her exploration. "You need to get out of that dress before this goes any further."

Accepting the challenge in his gaze, Louisa began to unbutton the bodice of her dress. When the last button was freed, she took a deep breath to calm her nerves and then shrugged her shoulders to free herself from the garment. With the fabric pooled at her hips, she shimmied herself free of it entirely. He scooped it up and then tossed it aside along with his clothing.

Layer by layer, she removed each item until she wore only her shift. Only then did he climb onto the bed with her, bearing her back onto the mound of pillows. When his lips closed over hers again, it was an entirely different thing. This wasn't simply a kiss, but an orchestrated and strategic assault. He seduced. Claimed. He was both generous and demanding at once. Thought fled entirely, and she could do nothing but give herself up to the sensations he stirred within her.

With skilled hands and expert lips, he brought her to the brink of madness, then beyond it. Waves of pleasure exploded within her. It was only then that he joined their bodies. There was a moment of discomfort, though she was so lost in the throes of her release it was barely noticeable. It was the intimacy of it, the vulnerability of giving herself to him entirely, that overwhelmed her. It was no longer just physical pleasure. There was a feeling of completeness she had never known before. But as before, he drove her to the brink of ecstasy, until she was all but mindless with it. She could do nothing then but lose herself in the pleasure he could give her—in the pleasure they could find together.

"THEY'VE CONSUMMATED THEIR marriage! You said it was to be in name only."

Fanny rolled over in his bed and looked at him with sleepy eyes. She was a sly creature. It was one of the reasons he had sent her to Rosehaven to sabotage his cousin's efforts to find a bride. "Explain to me how you misinterpreted that!" Terrence demanded of her.

"I never said it would be in name only. I said it would be a marriage of convenience. For one year. Then they would part ways," she insisted. "But he did tell her they would have no children."

Terrence frowned. "How, if they are going at one another like animals in rut, is that possible?"

"He said that precautions would be taken," Fanny insisted sitting up in the bed. Naked, she stretched to shamelessly accentuate her best assets—a pair of truly remarkable breasts.

Even as a man who had partaken in more than his fair share of carnal pursuits, it was an impressive sight. And a distracting one. After appreciating the view for a moment, Terrence tossed her dress at her. "Precautions? French letters fail. Withdrawal is hardly a guarantee. And none of that changes the fact that he's married her. The only way I get the money now is if he dies and I can be certain there is no heir in her belly!"

"You could always just kill them both," Fanny suggested.

Terrence didn't immediately discount the idea. It might well be his only real option. "I think the White Lady of Rosehaven needs to make another appearance. A more bold one this time. After all, everyone believes her presence is a harbinger of tragedy. What greater tragedy could there be than for a husband to be so overcome with jealousy that he kills his young bride and then himself?"

Fanny leaned back against the headboard. "You better marry me after all this. Who else would put up with your scheming and turned a blind eye while you tup every halfway pretty maid in the house?"

Terrence only smiled. He wouldn't marry her. Fanny would simply disappear like so many other young women did. Maids ran off all the time, after all. And he wasn't about to make an actress who'd slept with half the ne'er-do-wells in London the mistress of his home. But he needed her cooperation for a bit longer, and he'd let her keep her delusions to ensure her assistance.

"Get dressed so you can get to your room and change into your costume," he directed. "We've no time to waste."

Chapter Eleven

LOUISA COULDN'T SAY what it was that had awakened her. The room was dark. Douglas was still in the bed beside her, his breathing deep and even. Looking at him, she was so tempted to just lie there. But there was a sense of urgency that was undeniable.

Easing from the bed, she reached for her chemise and slipped it on. She'd been shameless enough already without parading around in the nude. Inexplicably drawn to the window, she looked out into the darkness of the garden beyond. Instantly, she knew where the sense of urgency had come from.

The white shrouded figure moved through the garden. The moon was bright, but not bright enough to see any details at such a distance. Just as before, it wandered along the garden paths to the lane, and then disappeared from sight. Turning away from the window, she gathered her dress but didn't bother with shoes. She was shrugging into the gown even as she slipped from the room. Padding down the corridor barefoot, she would have to be quick if she had any hope of catching up to whomever was impersonating the fabled ghost.

Rounding the corner to the stairs, Louisa drew up short. Terrence stood before her, a cruel smile playing about his lips.

"You know what they say about curiosity and cats, don't you, dear cousin?"

Louisa tried to hide the shiver that raced through her at the obvious threat in his words. "I certainly know what they say about every dog having his day."

That cold, bone-chilling grin on his face turned into a snarl. "You'll regret insulting me, Cousin Louisa. And it may well be the last thing you do."

She had no other warning. His hand snaked out, grabbing her upper arm and hauling her with him. But not down the stairs. Instead he pulled her to the opposite end of the corridor. The panic she'd felt at first began to fade and she struggled against him, even as she drew in a deep breath to scream for help.

He'd clearly guessed her intent, as he slammed her into the wall, pressing his hand over her mouth and nose. "Do not make a sound. I have a pistol in my pocket and I will shoot you without qualm. Then I will shoot Douglas. And there is no one in this house who would gainsay me . . . except for poor, dear Aunt Mary who's ready for Bedlam with all her talk of cards and crystals." Roughly, he released his hand.

"What do you mean to do with Douglas?"

"Nothing," he said. "So long as he doesn't manage to get himself another wife before the year is out. You see, that's the tricky wording of Uncle James's will. It doesn't matter who he's married to, or how many times he has married, so long as on the one-year anniversary of the reading of the will, Douglas has himself a wife. If he fails, then it becomes my turn. I'll have my chance at the family fortunes then."

"It was Fanny I saw in the garden. Wandering around in the dark wearing white like some sort of phantom, to scare away any poor superstitious village girl who might be tempted to ignore the family's dark history," Louisa surmised. It was a stalling tactic. He'd pushed her back against the wall, but there was a table beside her—a table bedecked with a small but heavy and very ornate candelabra. Fumbling for it, she finally managed to close her hand over it just as he abruptly let her go.

She could see him reaching for the gun in his pocket. It was her only chance. Swinging the candelabra upward, she caught his arm with it, the ornate scrollwork slicing his hand. Then she brought it crashing down again, this time against his forehead. Blood welled from the laceration instantly, running into his eyes.

Louisa scrambled away, screaming as she then ran down the corridor back to the room where she'd left Douglas sleeping. Even over her own ragged breathing and pounding heart, she could hear Terrence's heavy footfalls. She'd only managed to best him before because of luck and the element of surprise. That would no longer be on her side. With no other choice, Louisa screamed for all she was worth.

DOUGLAS SAT UP with a jolt. He wasn't immediately certain what had awakened him, but he was instantly aware of one thing. He was alone. Louisa was no longer in the bed beside him.

Something else penetrated the haze of sleep. The air around him was freezing cold. So cold that he could see his breath. Instantly, memories of Louisa's description of her encounters with Caroline came to mind.

"Are you here?" he whispered.

There was no sound, only the opening of the outer door to their chamber. It was a clear indication that he should follow. Feeling both foolish and afraid, he rose from the bed. Moving quickly, he grabbed his trousers and struggled into them. Shirtless and in his bare feet, he ran into the corridor. He could see Louisa running toward him, and chasing after her was a bloodied Terrence.

Caroline had warned him. She had warned him to spare Louisa the same fate she had suffered.

Rushing forward, Douglas grabbed her, pushing her behind him. He could see Terrence brandishing the pistol, but when he saw

Douglas, Terrence abruptly stopped. When Terrence raised his hand, leveling the pistol, Douglas knew he meant to fire. He would kill him, and then he would kill Louisa. Unwilling to let that happen, Douglas did the only thing he could. When he saw the minute flinch in Terrence's hand, just before the other man squeezed the trigger, he threw himself back against the wall, dragging Louisa with him.

The shot went wide. Without giving Terrence the chance to reload or fish the matching pistol from his pocket, Douglas launched himself at the other man, tackling him to the carpeted floor.

It seemed that Terrence lacked the skills to do battle with another man, someone who could match him in strength. His cousin apparently only ever engaged in violence against those who were weaker than himself.

Drawing his fist back, he hit Terrence again and again. Only when Terrence stopped moving entirely did he manage to pull himself back from that brink, back from allowing the damnable Blackwell temper to drive him to murder.

Turning to Louisa, he said, "Rouse a servant and send for the magistrate."

She nodded mutely and then stumbled toward the stairs on unsteady legs. He wanted to call her back. She was in no condition for such things, but he could hardly leave her alone with Terrence, even though he was unconscious at present. There was no way to know how long he would remain that way.

A pained groan from his cousin only confirmed it was the right choice. When Terrence's eyes opened, Douglas hauled him up by his coat and the used Terrence's own bloody cravat to bind his hands. "You'll hang for what you've done."

"What did I do other than have a midnight tryst with your bird that got slightly out of hand?" Terrence demanded, pausing to spit blood from his mouth. "Do you really want all of England to know what a trollop you've married?"

"It has nothing to do with Louisa," Douglas said. "And everything to do with Caroline. You killed her because I meant to marry her. Because Uncle James would have written you out of his will entirely then."

Terrence laughed. "You'll never be able to prove it."

"I don't need to." With grim satisfaction, Douglas explained, "You'll be in the local gaol until the next assizes. And by then, Uncle James's will, with all of its contingencies, will have been met. You'll be both penniless and disgraced. And I will have just cause to deny you entrance to Rosehaven ever again. No doubt Fanny will be less than enamored with you once your every avenue to the Blackwell family fortune has been closed. She might even be persuaded to testify against you."

There was a flicker of fear in Terrence's gaze then, the realization that all his scheming had been for naught. He was on the cusp of losing everything. "I'll go. I'll leave here, and you can have the bloody fortune!"

"That isn't good enough. Caroline deserves justice. I failed to protect her in life, but I will not betray her again in her death."

Epilogue

October 1st, 1832

IT WAS WELL into the evening by the time they returned from the assizes in Ashford. Just over a month since the constables had taken both Terrence and Fanny into custody. The servants were abuzz with the gossip. They had both been found guilty of their respective crimes. Terrence was to face transportation, and Fanny was sentenced to a seven-year term in prison for her role as a conspirator.

Mary felt vindicated, per her own report, stating that she had always thought poor Caroline's demise had resulted from something far more nefarious than a mere riding accident. And, of course, her cards had told her that it would happen just so. Or so she informed them dramatically as she sailed from the room with a swish of her heavily flounced skirts.

"Why did the magistrate and the judge keep talking about all the tragedy wrought by this wretched place?" Louisa asked as soon as the door closed.

Douglas's glance at her revealed far more than he had intended. She knew instantly that he didn't want to tell her. It was evident in his expression, in his posture, in the very air around him.

"You can tell me," she urged. "After everything I shared with you, knowing how positively hysterical it sounded, you have to know that you can trust me as I trusted you."

"It's not the same thing at all, Louisa," he said softly. "You were worried about me thinking you mad. I'm worried about you thinking me a murderer. That's what everyone believes all Blackwell men to be—past, present, and future."

She said nothing, just waited patiently for him to continue. After a long sigh, he did.

"My father murdered my mother. Much like Caroline's death, it was made to look like an accident. A fall down the stairs. But I saw it all. I know what he did. He pushed her in the middle of an argument, and she fell to her death. It was never proven, never taken to trial. But everyone knows. Then there is my grandfather who buried three wives, all of them under mysterious circumstances. That is how he amassed the Blackwell fortune. There's blood on every groat."

"They are not you," Louisa said simply.

"How can you be sure that I will not turn just as they did?"

"Because you have integrity, Douglas. You are not capable of such wickedness. If you were, you'd have continued to let the world think Caroline's death was an accident just to spare the family more scandal. Truth and justice mean more to you than personal gain."

"I want her to be at peace," he said softly. "I cared for her very deeply. But I wasn't in love with her . . . not as she loved me. I've felt guilty about that for years."

Louisa looked down at her clasped hands. "Perhaps you would have grown to love her as she loved you."

"I don't think so. Certainly there was affection and a kind of love. But loving someone and being in love with them—that is something entirely different." He paused then, looking away thoughtfully. "No, I was meant for something else."

"For the army? The life of a soldier?" Louisa asked. Though she smiled, it felt as if her heart was breaking. She'd made the terrible mistake of falling in love with him. It had been a valiant fight to keep her feelings contained, but she had failed pitifully. And in eleven months, he would send her away.

"No. The army wasn't my purpose. Just a distraction. It allowed me to escape the gossip and conjecture of this place. To go where no one knew my family history and expected me to turn into a monster."

She looked up then, meeting his gaze steadily. "Was I destined to become a fallen woman just because my mother had?"

His eyes widened with shock. "Of course, not. And women do not fall alone. There is always a dishonorable man somewhere within their stories. Someone who made promises they had no intention of keeping."

"I know something about that," she said. "I made promises to myself that I have not kept." And all of them had involved shielding her heart from him, of keeping some kind of distance between them.

"What does that mean?"

"I promised that I would guard my feelings, that I would not form any sort of attachment to you. Because we will part at some point, and I have no wish to have my heart broken. That is why I think we should go back to our separate chambers. I can return to the room I stayed in when I first arrived."

He shook his head. "No. I don't want that. I want you with me, Louisa,"

"I can't. I am not Caroline. I cannot love you and have only a pale glimmer of affection in return," she admitted.

⁂

HE HADN'T DARED hope. Not really. Even without her confession, he'd known that when their year was through, he would not give her up. Louisa had invaded his thoughts. His heart. She had burrowed into his very soul, it seemed.

"And why would you think that you do not have my love? I think perhaps you've had it from the moment I first saw you. Hatton had his way after all. He'd had it in mind all along that I should have a love match," he confessed. "So he found the one woman in all of England, perhaps in all the world, that I would never be able to resist."

Douglas watched her, analyzing every flicker of emotion on her face. There were many. Despair, hope, longing, tenderness—and perhaps that was what love truly was. It wasn't a single emotion but the presence of every emotion, swirling in a storm created by one person. Louisa could make him feel everything, and he had hope that perhaps he was that to her, as well.

"I thought I could resist you, too. That I could guard my heart well enough to keep you from stealing it." His mouth twisted in a rueful grin on that admission.

"I didn't steal it," she protested. "It was an even exchange. I took yours, but I gave you my own in return."

"Stay with me, Louisa."

"For the next eleven months?"

"Yes . . . and then for every month after. I never want to part from you. And I say to you something that I have never said to another woman. I do not just love you. I am in love with you. Hopelessly and permanently."

She smiled despite the tears glistening in her eyes. "How convenient it is that I feel exactly the same, and that I have no intention of going anywhere."

With a flick of his fingers, he locked the door behind him, and then Douglas held out his hand to her. And when she came to him, he showed her in every way that he could just how deeply he loved her and how much he wanted her.

The End

Author's Note

The village of Pluckley in Kent is reputed to be the most haunted village in England. The pseudo haunting perpetrated by the villains this story is an homage to the legend of the Lady of Rose Court. And Caroline's ghost was a sad one for me, but it is purely fictitious. There is nothing in the many paranormal tales from Pluckley that relates to her tragic tale. But I like to think that after she saved Louisa and her killer was brought to justice that she found her own sort of peace. If you'd like to read more about Pluckley's ghostly inhabitants, a simple Google search will result in a wealth of information.

Thank you for reading, and I hope you enjoyed my contribution to this ghostly collection.

Chasity Bowlin

About the Author

Chasity Bowlin lives in central Kentucky with her husband and their menagerie of animals. She loves writing, loves traveling and enjoys incorporating tidbits of her actual vacations into her books. She is an avid Anglophile, loving all things British, but specifically all things Regency.

Growing up in Tennessee, spending as much time as possible with her doting grandparents, soap operas were a part of her daily existence, followed by back to back episodes of Scooby Doo. Her path to becoming a romance novelist was set when, rather than simply have her Barbie dolls cruise around in a pink convertible, they time traveled, hosted lavish dinner parties and one even had an evil twin locked in the attic.

Website: www.chasitybowlin.com

Made in the USA
Columbia, SC
11 April 2025